Lukewarm September

Lukewarm September

Anna-Stina Johansson

She was pleased that her psychiatrist had followed her here. On the other hand, Pamela thought as she reached for the door handle, that this was the least Ms. Hayes could do. This was her idea, after all. She hesitated, the door still safely closed. Why had she let Ms. Hayes talk her in to this? Okay, she knew she needed help to cure her social phobia but never in a million years had she thought she would end up doing this!

Her hand trembled as she opened the door. The first thing she noticed was a sign, "No shoes in the Dojo". Ms. Hayes followed her in; they took off their shoes and chatted quietly with each other until a man in his mid-thirties came towards them, smiling. Pamela looked down. Maybe it was he who had sent her the information via email.

"Who was it that you have been in contact with?" Ms. Hayes asked.

"Somebody named Luke." Pamela didn't look up.

"Well that's me, I'm sempai Luke." He gave her a grin. "You must be Pamela, right?"

"Yes, that's me." She could feel her burning cheeks; she could have fried on egg on them.

Luckily, Luke started talking again because she hated awkward silences. He explained a little about Karate Kyokushinkai and that they practiced every Monday and Thursday from 7:30 pm to 9:00 pm. "There are too few interested at this time to start a beginner's group but you are more than welcome to practice with us." He gave her a friendly smile. "It will be tough for you since you're the only beginner but it's not impossible."

Pamela swallowed. Did she want to become well or not? She decided to grasp the nettle. "When can I start?"

"Now."

"No. Not immediately!"

He laughed heartily. " Oh I see, you need to be prepared mentally. What about this Thursday then?"

"Okay."

"Good! Feel free to stay and watch while we practice," he said and then he left.

Ms. Hayes had told her that this would be a great opportunity for Pamela to get rid of all her fears. She was absolutely convinced that Pamela would feel safer and get better self-confidence if she could protect herself. Pamela had reluctantly admitted that a long time ago she had had a desire to learn some kind of martial art but never thought that she would be strong enough to do it.

The following Thursday her pony tail swayed back and forth as she slowly entered the dojo. She had thought of this evening with delight mingled with terror! She wore a blue t-shirt and black trousers since she was a novice. All the others had their white suits on but with different colored belts. The belts showed what grade they had. She didn't have time to think any more of that before the training started. Pamela got confused right away since sempai Luke talked Japanese. She had studied the papers he had given her and thought she understood it fairly well, but following a foreign language there was another question. With fifteen people in the room speaking Japanese she felt like a fool although languages had never been a problem for her. Contrarily, she had been a straight A student in her German and Spanish classes.

Worst was when sempai Luke told them to do sit ups and count to ten on Japanese while they were doing it. Oh dear God! When she heard the others count she started to feel desperate trying to

remember the numbers on the paper! Oh

no, it was soon her turn! How could

someone come up with a crazy exercise like

this! Doing sit ups and counting in

Japanese!

"Ichi, Ni, San, Shi..." and that was as far as

she came. Way too much to do at the same

time! The people in the group were in

different ages and she definitely felt like a

fool when twelve years old boys were

better than her. Then finally Luke said that

she could count in English.

"Five… six…" Oh dear, I think I have forgotten my own language too!

"Seven…eight…nine, ten" Phew, that was a frightening experience! But she smiled triumphantly. She had survived!

Then they began to practice punches and kicks. Pamela thought that she must have lost her head when she agreed to join this group! It was too confusing for her to try to do what he demonstrated and to understand the new words! All this new information spun round and round in her head. Did this man think that she could be his reflection? Had he no understanding that it was hard to copy someone else's movements? It would have been so much easier if she could have stood behind him instead of facing him as he told her what to do. Indeed her brain didn't seem to want to cooperate with her tonight. She couldn't even understand left and right any longer.

Luke had obviously noticed that she had trouble following him. For a second she thought that she would stop breathing when he touched her. He was close now.

"Keep your arm like this." He bent her arm a little bit. "Remember to keep your arm slightly bent like this otherwise you will hurt yourself when you hit someone."

Pamela just nodded. What the heck was he doing?

With a twinkle in his eye he carefully curved her fingers to a closed fist.

She didn't dare to breath. She couldn't believe that she was able to enjoy a man's presence that much!

"Keep it like this." He leaned forward. His beard-stubble almost touched her cheek.

"By the way, you're doing well."

She smiled. Suddenly it wasn't only the training that made her warm.

Luke turned to the entire group and pointed to a place in the end of the dojo. "Lie down closely together on your backs here."

Pamela's palms started sweating. What were they going to do now?

Of course there were just a few other women there, but they had higher grades than her, meaning that Pamela, who was at the bottom of the hierarchy, had no other choice than to lie down next to a young man. That was beyond scary for her!

Luke looked at the group. "Now we're going to walk on each other's tummies." He was the first one to do it and when he had walked over all of them he lay down very close to Pamela. She hadn't seen this was coming! If she had understood that there would have been that much body contact she would have thought twice before she said yes to this. She felt like she was going to die when some of the other men stepped on her tummy! Then it was her turn and she didn't enjoy it one bit to walk barefoot on the others! She couldn't have been in full possession of all her senses when she said yes to karate!

They repeated this exercise a few times and each time Luke lay down close to her, once he even twisted his feet around hers which almost gave Pamela a heart attack! Why is he doing that for? Did he think that she would run away or what? At the same time she admitted that it felt quite nice to have him that close.

When the training was over she went to the entrance to put on her jacket, socks and shoes. She felt someone behind her and turned around.

Luke smiled at her. "May I walk you home?"

"You don't…"

"I won't take no for an answer."

"So why did you ask then?"

He couldn't help but laugh. "I thought you would say yes since I've been flirting with you all night long but it seems like you play hard to get."

"Well, if you only knew! That's not the case

at all." She looked down.

He lifted gently up her chin and forced her to meet his gaze. "What is the case then?"

"That's a long story"

He winked at her. "I got all the time in the world for you, baby."

Pamela couldn't help but wonder if her face was as red as a tomato now. "Are you nuts?"

A wide grin spread over his face.

"Absolutely not, why do you wonder?"

"Because of the things you just told me."

"What about them?"

"You're absolutely crazy coming on to me like this! Can't you see that I'm dripping with sweat?"

He gave her a mischievous smile. "All I can see is that you are very attractive."

Pamela was speechless. Luke just smiled, grabbed her by the hand and opened the door. Then they left the dojo closely together and stepped into the lukewarm September night.